500 YEARS OF TRAGEDY

The site of Cartagena.
A history of bravery, sea battles,
sieges, greed and shame.
The history of El Darién.

By

Santiago Martínez Concha

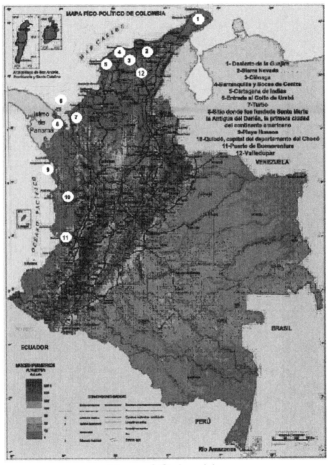

Map of Colombia

A faithful recognition to the
conquerors and heroes
of our past, among them:
Rodrigo de Bastidas,
Vasco Núñez de Balboa,
Blas de Lezo y Olavarrieta
the greatest of sea heroes
of all times.

FOREWORD

Tf C

1

When the first Bondawé Abundá arrived in Chocó, he came with the chains of hate, and sadness tying his feet and hands to his soul. He was like an ebony giant and the chaplain of the port who baptized him, not understanding his name called him Barnabas and so he stayed. The Spanish trafficker who razed his fishing village on the coast of Dakar left behind only desolation and death and abandoned nets in the sand with fish still entangled in them among the gullies of seagulls.

Chained to his wife, after a long sea voyage in the lower part of a galleon where they managed to survive diseases, excrement, urine, blood, sweat and rats, one in two blacks died in that travel. Once they arrived in the New World, they were sold to the highest bidder in the market of Santa María la Antigua del Darién, the first newly founded city on the American continent by Vasco Núñez de Balboa 5 centuries before, there in 1513. -Although there was another one year older called San Sebastian, nobody remembers it-. They were lucky that the same owner bought them both. Since then their lives and those of their descendants would be planted in that new land for five hundred years until one of them would be sold to a merchant in Santa Marta, the second oldest city on the continent, founded in 1525 by the conqueror Rodrigo de Bastidas. A century later another would be sold in Cartagena de Indias in 1630 and from all these came the Barnabas Abundá, and their hundreds of descendants, one of whom is here, in this story. A history of violence and oblivion, with a memory lost among the jungles of the coast. Over time, to differentiate themselves from each other, the Barnabas Abundá were baptized and added to their names that of Joseph, John, Jesus, Trinity, John, Mary, and the Blessed Sacrament, but they all kept proud, in one way or another, the history of their origins.

2

The Colombian north coast over the Atlantic Ocean and the western coast over the Pacific Ocean, it's the story of two coasts of the same country whipped by pain, although, the north coast has been favored by wealth, the west coast has remained poor and covered with oblivion. While countries in the center of the continent such as Bolivia or Paraguay would give anything to get an exit to the sea, many do not know that Colombia has access to the two largest oceans on the planet: the Atlantic and the Pacific. Unfortunately, guerrillas, oblivion, ignorance and injustice have done their part, but despite all the vicissitudes, the time has come to be reborn! Here the links with Spain, the mother country, are revealed from beginning to end.

Spain's effort was impressive, which, although it made mistakes, also extended and built a great empire beyond the sea. The bravery, determination and retinue of the Spanish soldier became legendary in America and when we see the works and monuments he left, we can only admire that ingenious and tough peninsular race that populated the continent, mixing with his natives and with the blacks brought from Africa.

One of the richest Colombian states in gold, silver and platinum, as well as the biodiversity of its natural resources, the largest on the planet, is Chocó, which also owns the Atrato River, the deepest in the world. The first settlers that arrived there were the Barnabas Abundá, to an imposing river where blood flowed like in any other of the great rivers around the planet. A river that in its average is also the deepest. The river is born in the municipality of Caramanta in the Western Cordillera of Los Andes and with just 750 kilometers of route it reaches 150 rivers and 3,000 streams, with an average depth ranging between 31 and 32 m and a width that fluctuates between 500 m and 1 km, in one of the wettest areas of the planet. It is said that to smoke a cigar there is first necessary to toast it. I know, I've been there.

The flow of the river is so great that with it all the reservoirs of Colombia could be filled in a little more than 14 days. The history of this river, which not everyone knows and many forget, is plagued by violence since Balboa explored it just 10 kilometers from its mouth in 1511, a couple of years before the founding of

Santa María la Antigua del Darién. It is a wild land with a small population of about 35,000 indigenous people who make up a little less than 9% of the total and the rest are mostly black occupying 88%, However, there also inhabit some foreigners, mestizos, whites, guerrilla and paramilitary groups completing the population chart with a scarce 3% remaining. Unfortunately, the same happens with violent groups as when a drop of oil touches the water: it spreads occupying a large space on the surface and in this case, that drop of oil is a murder or a crime against humanity which produces the terror, insecurity and fear around you like a large oil stain on the surface of the water, spreading more and more, as these violent acts increase.

The name of the river was perhaps given by Dutch and English merchants and smugglers who crossed it in the sixteenth and seventeenth centuries, calling it the "Rio de la Trata", which derived over the years in Río Atrato. But not only merchants and smugglers crossed the river, but also privateers looking for gold, silver and platinum. The so-called 'gold route' is a partially cobbled and tortuous road built with the Spanish effort, the blood and sweat of black slaves brought from Africa, one of them Barnabas Abundá, helped unite a small port established since the time of the conquest over the Atrato River called Vigia del Fuerte with the Pacific Ocean. He was a big and noble black and soon earned the nickname: "giant."

The Atrato was closed to river traffic for several centuries, under penalty of death, by the zeal of the Spanish kings to preserve its wealth for the crown and perhaps this is due, in addition to the weather and greed, its backwardness and obliviousness until today. The river runs from south to north, with 508 km navigable by vapors from its mouth to Quibdó, the capital of the current Department, in a delta formed by 7 arms that embrace the Caribbean Sea like an octopus without wanting to release it. It is like a gigantic and mysterious snake that moves slowly, between cliffy banks until it reaches the sea. A geographer called it a "movable lagoon" and another a "cursed river", with an Indian and black population constantly threatened by guerrillas, countless snakes and poisonous animals, tropical diseases including malaria, yellow fever, vampires and the floods.

Its flow is so immense, that there has been talk many times about the construction of an interoceanic canal that connects the Atrato River with the Pacific Ocean which would be a waterway with better characteristics than those of Panama, but so far everything is studies, false hopes and promises for a native population increasingly decimated by the demon of deception, disappointment, greed and poverty.

The fine fast-hulled vessels of the French fishermen and smugglers, as well as the 'customs', pirates and privateers, were often paired with sails to the third, rigging which was also called 'quechemarín'. Giving them great agility in their turn and assault maneuvers, and it was in one of these that a descendant of Barnabas Abundá was taken to Cartagena de Indias. All kinds of sails propelled large and small ships along the Atrato River, and when blacks or Indians saw them from a distance they knew that there was another smuggler or a privateer willing to do anything to obtain gold or blacks to exchange them or resell them in the markets of Jamaica, Cartagena, or further north.

At the end of the 17th century, the French government promoted the creation of a commercial company that would sail the Caribbean and the Darién called the Company of Santo Domingo, in order to improve the economic and demographic situation of its Caribbean colony. However, the island of Santo Domingo and particularly the so-called "band of the South", housed the Brotherhood of the Coast, a name given as a crossing point and meeting of Dutch, English and French pirates and smugglers. From there, the crews with different flags attacked the Spanish coast and ships, built outposts in the Darien and made contact with the local indigenous population.

The establishment of the French colonial government in Santo Domingo in 1664, did not pose a threat to the groups of pirates and smugglers who actively participated in the assaults on Cartagena which began just 10 years after its foundation. The pirates already roamed the coast of the continent in search of fortune since then. In 1542, the French pirate Roberto Baal seized Cartagena, accompanied by four hundred and fifty men. A second attack was carried out in 1559, by another Frenchman, Martin Cote, who managed to take the city and rose with a swag. In 1568 the city was able to defend itself successfully, in front of Sir John Hawkins, an English nobleman famous for trading with slaves and bitter enemy of the Spanish crown. The English tried to enter the city by posing as a slave trader. The governor who suspected the worst did not allow him to enter and the city had to endure eight days of siege before the English gave up. But a terrible attack followed, one that would not forgive nuns, women or children. In 1586, the Englishman Francis Drake, took Cartagena de Indias between the months of February and April, occupying it for a hundred days and settling in the governorate. Once he managed to penetrate the city, he caused numerous fires, destruction and looting everywhere, even in the Cathedral he incurred horrendous sacrificial excesses with women and enormous destruction. Only after receiving a large ransom did he agree to leave the city. All these assaults occurred with relative ease, as the city was not yet fortified. The Castle of San Felipe, the walls and other forts would begin to be built from then on. However, another pirate attack was carried out in 1685, by the famous Henry Morgan. Their cannons shot down one of the towers of the Santo Domingo's church where José Barnabas Abundá, great-great grandson of Jesús Barnabas Abundá and his family had hidden that afternoon from the bombing. That attack would also cause huge destruction and countless fires, including those of a cloister inhabited by nuns and orphans where few were saved. José Barnabas proved that day to be a brave man, went out to the street to pick up wounded and orphans and began to take them to the church to be healed, work that earned him to be taken into account by the mayor of Cartagena to continue serving as a soldier at King's orders.

Just 12 years later, on April 13, 1697, the Baron of Pointis arrived in Cartagena de Indias with a large fleet that would begin to bomb the city the next day. The Baron acted under the orders of the King of France and attacked Cartagena with a force of over 4000 men, mostly mercenaries collected in Cuba and the Dominican Republic. He knew perfectly the disposition of the military system and the fortifications, which is a very well-done spying activity, without no one knowing with certainty who had sold the plans of the fortified city to the French. After several battles won and an attempt to negotiate with the governor, the French were forced to leave because of the yellow fever, which decimated the invading troops and offered a more effective resistance than that of the locals. However, the Caribbean mercenaries, immune to the epidemic, managed to carry out considerable looting.

The first action of the Baron de Pointis was to land on the Island of "Tierrabomba"! with all its filibusters to attack the Castle of San Luis de Bocachica, defended by Don Sancho Ximeno, a man of immense courage who would repeal the attack to be then betrayed by his own men, mostly black slaves, who, enveloped by the terror inspired by the buccaneers and the noise of the cannons, carabiners and halberds, took advantage of the first opportunity they had to deliver their weapons and open the doors of the Castle to the French. One of them, Barnabas Trinidad Abundá, a tall and stocky young man, being 15 years old strongly opposed their action, and at the risk of losing his life, attacked one of the leaders by sticking a knife in the middle of his chest that broke his heart, but it was useless. The doors opened and the defenders in command of Don Sancho Ximeno surrendered. Pointis, like a great gesture of gallantry, recognized the commander's courage, handing him his sword while saying: "A knight like you should not be unarmed." The news of the young negro's action reached his ears, and after the battle passed, he was incorporated as his personal assistant, while his father José Abundá was still serving as a free slave incorporated into the king's militia. The French made their way to the city and took the impressive and almost impregnable Castillo de San Felipe de Barajas, whose construction began on the hill of San Lázaro in 1536 and was completed a little more than three decades later in 1698, a year later of the assault. From there they mercilessly fired the Half Moon Gate until they opened a gap through which they entered, seizing the suburb of Gethsemane, but not before fighting the last defenders who still guarded the site, killing all those who failed to hide or fled from that hell. The only one who did not flee was José Abundá, who remained there in the midst of smoke and dead bodies, until a piece of lead fired by a carabiner went to be embedded in the middle of his forehead, killing him on the spot.

The history of the Castillo de San Felipe is closely linked to Cartagena. After the capture by Pointis and several pirates' assaults, another 55 pieces were added to the scarce eight original cannons to complete a total of 63 guns with their corresponding body of gunners. At least seven batteries were built: San Lázaro, Santa Bárbara, the Redemption, San Carlos, the Apostles, the Cross and the Hornabeque, all strategically distributed. The walls were made obliquely, impossible to climb and the main access was made through a small ramp easy to defend. The interior of the castle is full of tortuous and mysterious tunnels, some so long that reach 600 m in length. There is also a cistern, a Santa Barbara or ammunition depot and an enclosure to house about 300 people. It is a majestic structure that dominates the landscape of the bay, the most important made by Spain in the Americas, and its walls cut with great symmetry and its mortar mixed with the blood of animals and slaves, after five centuries it won a position like the eighth wonder of Colombia.

After ratifying the capitulation with of Cartagena of Cartagena de Indias' authorities, Pointis entered the city triumphantly and attended a Thanksgiving Te-Deum that he himself ordered to be celebrated in the Cathedral. The invaders would be almost a month in the city, during which time they robbed and looted all the inhabitants at their leisure, committed excesses, raped many of their women, including the exaggerated case of some who were raped on the tables from the altars, they desecrated the temples and stole jewels and religious treasures of great value, thus violating the terms of the capitulation. Pointis left Cartagena de Indias on July 1, 1697, betraying and leaving behind a squad of his pirates staying with the part of the loot agreed with them, which is why they returned on what was left of the city and finished looting it , taking at least two million pesos in gold and sowing desolation and bitterness behind it. Nothing was saved! That huge sum that the pirates took, contrasts with the 13,235 pesos in gold that was the cost of the construction of the Castillo de San Felipe for almost 30 years.

In 1741, after the declaration of the war between England and Spain, Admiral Edward

Vernon was ordered to attack Cartagena. With a fleet of 186 ships and 27,600 men - other sources speak of 25,000 and even 23,000 -, the Admiral intended to bend "Half-man", also called "Patepalo" - Stick leg - Don Blas de Leso and Olavarrieta, military Spanish veteran who had lost an eye, an arm and a leg in different battles in Europe. He would be the man in charge to erase the defeat of the Battle of the "Invincible Armada" of King Philip II of Spain, against the English fleet of Elizabeth I of England in 1588, just over a century earlier. The hostilities that began in 1585 ended with the Treaty of London of 1604, one that was favorable to Spain. However, there are some errors and inaccuracies that have arisen during the last centuries in relation to the "Invincible Armada", with own exaggerations also born during the Victorian era whose purpose was to add coal to the bonfire of the "Black Legend" against Spain. But now let's turn our eyes back to Cartagena and the magnificent defense that took place in that year of 1741.

No one, absolutely no one over the centuries has more courage and is not bigger as a sea warrior than Blas de Lezo and Olavarrieta, born in Pasajes, on February 3, 1689 - in Guipúzcoa - in Euskera -, which is a Spanish province and historical territory of the autonomous community of the Basque Country-, and died in Cartagena de Indias, in Nueva Granada, on September 7, 1741, just under 4 months after the Cartagena' site was completed, with 52 years of age. He did not die from any of his injuries but was defeated by the plague that was generated with the decomposed bodies of thousands of mostly English bodies and mercenaries hooked by Admiral Vernon in Jamaica.

Admiral Edward Vernon was born in Westminster, London, on November 12, 1684 and would die in Necton, Suffolk, at age 73 - advanced age for that time - on October 30, 1757. Vernon was the English naval officer who lost the site of Cartagena de Indias in 1741 and with-it England would lose supremacy over the seas for more than half a century. His first actions took place in the framework of the War of Spanish Succession, where he participated in the battles of Malaga and Barcelona - in 1704 and 1705.

In 1720 he was appointed Commodore of Port Royal on the island of Jamaica. In November 1739, at the outbreak of the Seat War - or Jenkins Ear War - Vernon was appointed commander in chief of all British naval forces in the West Indies.

His first action in that war was the looting and destruction of Portobelo, a poorly defended Panamanian port that was part of the route followed by the Spanish fleet. Portobelo was particularly important at that time for the realization of a famous annual fair to which Chocó's gold and the silver extracted from the Potosí mines in Bolivia and Peru arrived. From there the ships departed for Spain following the route of the island of Cuba, avoiding other very dangerous routes in seas infested with pirates. The capture of Portobelo was the cause of the boasting and subsequent conceit of Vernon, as the triumph was greatly exaggerated by the English who gave themselves to all kinds of celebrations and made numerous tributes to the admiral, who turned ipso facto into a national hero. King George II himself attended a gala dinner held in his honor in 1740, during which the current British national anthem, God Save the King was first presented as part of these celebrations and the patriotic song Rule Britannia was also created! The exaggeration reached the point that two streets were named, one in London and one in Dublin, with the names of Portobello Road. But such celebration's euphoria and conceit would cost the English dearly that they would be humiliated by "Mediohombre" -Half-man-, Don Blas de Lezo and Olavarrieta with 52 years. While in 1741, Vernon, 57, would lead to defeat one of the largest naval fleets in history until the invasion of Normandy in 1944 two centuries later.

Always, de Lezo was linked to the water and the sea and as sometimes happens, this inheritance was carried in his blood: his ancestors were linked to it the same as the people who saw him born. There are not enough words to praise this 'Half-man', experienced sailor, intelligent, recursive and brave like none. Neither history nor Spain will ever see a sailor with greater courage than this, worthy of being among the best of all time in the annals of the sea. It is a pity that his name is a bit lost and forgotten over the centuries.

When Blas de Lezo with only 33 years arrived in Cartagena in 1737 as General Commander of that city, he had already fought in 22 battles in Europe and the Mediterranean and emerged victorious in most of them. He arrived with the ships, Fuerte and Conquistador and would defend the city in 1741 from a siege with the attack by the English admiral Edward Vernon who expected to subjugate it. The pretext of the English to start the conflict with Spain was that the ship's captain Juan Leon Fandiño seized the corsair ship commanded by Robert Jenkins near the coast of Florida. and he cut off an ear to his captain while telling him - according to the testimony of the same Englishman:

"Go and tell your king that I will do the same to him if he dares the same."

In his appearance before the House of Lords, Jenkins denounced the fact with a flask in his hand, which contained his ear preserved in alcohol. This served for the English to call the conflict the "Jenkins' Ear War." The English considered this an offense to the king of England and sent Edward Vernon to suppress the offense.

Vernon in a burst of euphoria after the looting of the poorly trimmed Portobelo square in Panama, challenged de Lezo, to which the Spanish sailor replied:

"If I had been in Portobelo, I would not have your Merced -Lord- insulted the places of King my Lord with impunity, because the spirit that was lacking in Portobelo would have been enough for me to contain your cowardice."

In this fight of crossed destinations between Spain and England, each power would gain a great victory and supremacy over the sea for some time. England in 1588 with the defeat of "the Invincible Armada", Spain in the

s. XVIII from 1741 with the triumph of Blas de Lezo and the defeat of Admiral Vernon, and England in the s. XIX from 1805 with the triumph in the battle of Trafalgar over the Franco-Spanish fleet, as we will see later:

The English fleet that participated in the capture of Cartagena de Indias in 1741, would be the largest group of warships that sailed the seas, except for the Allied fleet that took part in the Normandy's landing in 1944. Larger than the one which composed the famous "Invincible Armada" of Felipe II - term coined by the English in 1588- with the purpose of dethroning Queen Elizabeth I of England-, and invading that country, which was destroyed, among other things, by a storm due to the trade winds, forcing it to face the cliffs of the English coast.

The Vernon fleet had 2,000 guns arranged on 186 ships, including warships, frigates, brulotes and transport ships, and 23,600 combatants among sailors, soldiers and black slaves "macheteros" of Jamaica, plus 4,000 Virginia recruits under the orders of Lawrence Washington, half-brother of the future liberator George Washington, and surpassed in more than 60 ships the Great Navy of Philip II.

The unquestionable strategic merit of victory has no discussion or doubt in the annals of America and the world. With scarce 2,800 men - other sources speak of 3,600- among regular troops, militiamen, 600 Indian "flecheros" -arrow-men- brought from the interior, plus the sailors and landing troops of the only six warships available to the city.

Vernon's squad had departed from Port Royale in Jamaica and anchored in early March 1741 off the coast of Cartagena de Indias, the most important city in the Caribbean, to which all merchandise from commerce between Spain and the Indies arrived, including the treasures extracted from the silver mines of Potosí in Bolivia and the silver mines of Peru. The great British fleet was sighted on March 13, 1741, which put the city on guard, which had already been alerted in advance, thanks to the Spanish crown spies, about the future attack of the English admiral.

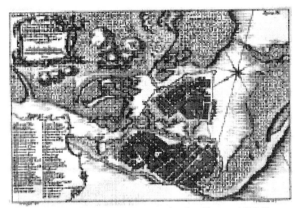

Map of Cartagena de Indias, 1535

___Up: Attack to Fuerte de San José
___Down: Attack to Castillo de Bocachica

Before preparing to disembark, Vernon silenced the batteries of the fortresses of Chamba, San Felipe and Santiago. Then he prepared to gun the fortress of San Luis de Bocachica day and night for sixteen days. Bocachica was defended by Carlos Desnaux with 500 men who, finally, had to retreat to the offensive superiority of the English fleet. After this fortress only the Fortress of Bocagrande remained as entrance to the bay. In the first, four Spanish ships were destroyed to prevent the navigation of the narrow canal and, in the second, two additional ships, against Blas de Lezo's opinion that it would not serve much after what was seen in Bocachica, without being able to prevent access to the bay. Thus, de Lezo had sacrificed his ships without greater results. The blockade of the Bocagrande canal served almost nothing, as he had thought. After leaving the fortress of Bocagrande, all the Spanish defenders entrenched themselves in the Castle of San Felipe de Barajas. Vernon entered the bay triumphantly, believing that the victory was only a matter of a few days and sent an email to England giving part of the victory.

Next, he ordered an incessant cannon to the castle of San Felipe by sea and land to soften the forces of the garrison inside. There were only 600 men left under Lezo and Desnaux. Vernon then decides to surround the fortress and attack through its rear. For this he ordered his troops to enter the jungle, which was an odyssey for the British who contracted dysentery and malaria and lost hundreds of their men. However, they reached the fortress' gates and Vernon ordered to attack with all the force of his infantry. Barnabas of the Blessed Sacrament, a huge black man with a bright body like that of a panther, armed with a double-edged machete was placed in front of the defenders of the narrow access ramp to the castle, the only entrance to Lezo's fortress. He quickly ordered a plug of three hundred men armed with only white weapons, managing to contain the attack and causing 1500 casualties to the assailants. This incredible act, almost suicidal, reminds that of the Greek Leonidas in his defense of the "Pass of the Thermopylae" 1,800 years before, where we must also exalt his courage and the courage of all defenders, hence the title of the "Heroic" that Cartagena received, honoring the city. The morale of the attackers dropped considerably with this act and because of the epidemics and tropical diseases that caused continued casualties. Vernon faced for the first time the serious possibility of defeat, due to the impressive resistance of the Spanish soldiers, which far exceeded his expectations.

Unfortunately for him, by that time he had sent part of the victory to England. Vernon heatedly discussed with his generals the plan to follow and finally agreed to build stopovers and surprise defenders on the night of April 19. This decision would prove fatal to the assailants. Under General Woork, three columns of grenadiers and several redcoat companies were organized. Avant-garde were Jamaican slaves like cannon fodder, armed with a simple machete. The advance was slow due to the great weight of the artillery they carried and the continuous fire that came out of the trenches from the top of the fortress. Although Vernon's troops were exposed on a large esplanade, they managed to reach the walls. But Blas de Lezo, anticipating this attack, made a simple determination: he had ordered to dig a moat around the castle wall, so that the scales fell short to overcome the moat and the wall, leaving the attackers unprotected and not knowing what to do. The Spaniards, from above, continued with their large fire, which caused a spooky massacre in the invading ranks. At dawn on April 20, countless corpses were seen, wounded and mutilated around the fortress, revealing the very serious British defeat. The Spaniards, upon realizing it, took the opportunity to charge Bayonet causing the British to flee, managing to kill hundreds of them in the retreat, taking possession of the equipment left by the besiegers after the escape. Without fully accepting his defeat, Vernon had no choice but to retreat to the ships and ordered for thirty days plus a continuous cannon. However, illnesses and a shortage of supplies began to make a dent in what was left of his troops. Finally, the British High Command orders the withdrawal, slowly and incessantly of cannon. On April 30, the prisoner exchange took place. Like a dejected brave dog, giving its last barking and with its tail between its legs, the last ships departed on May 20, having to burn five of them for lack of crew

The British had between 8,000 and 10,000 dead and about 7,500 wounded, many of whom died on the way to Jamaica. In Cartagena the flower and cream of the British imperial official had died, in addition the attackers lost 1500 guns and innumerable mortars, shops and all kinds of equipment, with a balance of 17 seriously damaged warships, although none was lost. This was a serious setback for the imperial British war fleet, which was virtually dismantled and took a long time to recover.

But while Vernon retired like a wounded lion to lick his wounds, his victory was celebrated in Britain, for they did not yet know the disastrous end of this adventure. Up to eleven different types of commemorative medals and coins were minted extolling the capture of Cartagena by the 'Anglo-American' forces. One of them showed de Lezo - with two legs - kneeling before Vernon, handing him his sword and with the inscription "The pride of

Spain humiliated by Vernon." These came to circulate in Spain with the consequent humiliation and mockery that the English would suffer. Merchants by nature were ahead of the events and also made ceramic pipes with the flagship and the name of Vernon engraved on them, as well as fans, dishes and other utensils and hookahs. In 1742, Vernon, aware of the death of Blas de Lezo, rounded Cartagena again, but after thinking twice, he dared not attack, because he managed to think that a second defeat would have been for him more than unforgivable.

The British began to wonder when the ships commanded by their admiral-hero and his crew would return, and then the truth was discovered, so King George II, ashamed, forbade his chroniclers to make mention or write stories concerning the in fact, erasing it at a stroke, as if it had never happened - a clear press censorship as it would be called today-.

But you cannot cover the sun with your hands and that order would not be fully fulfilled. English historians, writers and cartographers made before and after maps and books, which were published in England itself. After two other failed attacks in Santiago de Cuba and Panama, Vernon was replaced by Chaloner Ogle and was forced to return to England in 1742 to communicate in his shame that Cartagena's victory never existed. Vernon's faint-hearted spirit became apparent by blaming General Wentworth, commanding the troops, of the disaster suffered in Cartagena. With these manipulations he was promoted in 1745 to Admiral of the North Sea fleet, however, the publication of two pamphlets revealing his disagreements with the Admiralty caused him to be expelled from the Navy in 1746. Years after his death in 1757, a nephew of his paid a monument in his honor at Westminster Abbey, whose epitaph reads the phrase "... and in

Cartagena conquered as far as the naval force could take the victory." A hollow phrase that fails to erase what happened, nor the medals minted in his honor. To this day many of his countrymen do not forgive him for defeat, the shame of deception and pain that caused them to suffer, and the odd tourist who knows the true façade of the false hero, when he arrives in Westminster, he can only smile for his in. While on his retreat, Admiral Vernon moved away from the bay with his shattered fleet shouting a phrase to the wind:

"God damn you, Lezo!" -Let God curse you Lezo! -.

This curse would unfortunately be fulfilled a little less than three months after the triumph, for de Lezo would die because of the plague unleashed by the thousands of bodies scattered in insecurity and decay. In a letter written to

Vernon after the defeat, Blas de Lezo wrote the immortal phrase:

"To come to Cartagena, it is necessary that the king of England builds another major squad because this one has only been left to drive coal from Ireland to London, which would have been better than undertaking a conquest he cannot achieve."

The war reported few successes and many problems to Great Britain, since the failure of Cartagena de Indias added several defeats when the British tried to take San Agustin in Florida, the port of La Guaira, Puerto Cabello, Guantanamo and Havana. However, the Spanish counterattack in the battle of Bloody Marsh – Pantano Sangriento - in Georgia, was repelled and therefore the fighting ended without border changes in America.

For its part Spain managed to maintain its territories, and prolong its military supremacy in

America, because as a result of this battle Spain strengthened control of its Empire in America for 70 years and with it the prolongation of maritime rivalry between Spaniards, French and British continued until the early nineteenth century. This was the biggest English defeat in the New World and one of the biggest in its history, as well as a great victory for Spain with a huge disproportion between the two sides. So colossal was the English defeat, which ensured the Spanish rule of the seas for 7 more decades, until it lost it in the famous battle of Cape Trafalgar in the Gulf of Cádiz in 1805 where the Napoleonic forces' navy lost with the Franco-Spanish coalition the battle against the navy of the English coalition, in the most important battle of the s. XIX, which, on the part of the English, was commanded by Admiral Lord Horatio Nelson aboard his flagship ship HMS Victoria. Of it, among many other things, we have the wonderful paintings and watercolors of William Turner with atmospheres burning with light.

But now returning to our history of the Cartagena's site 56 years earlier, for the United Kingdom, the consequences of Vernon's defeat in the medium term were devastating. Thanks to this victory over the British, Spain was able to maintain territories and a network of military installations in the Caribbean and the Gulf of Mexico that would be masterfully used by Lt. Col. Bernardo de Galvez to play a decisive role in the independence of the British colonies of North America, during the so-called American War of Independence, in 1776. The War of the Seat would be merged later in the War of Austrian Succession, so that Great Britain and Spain did not sign the peace until the Treaty of Aachen, in 1748.

From Blas de Lezo the American continent could see their descendants. On May 5, 1725

Blas Fernando de Lezo y Pacheco, first Marquis of Oviedo married in Lima with the Creole lady Josefa Pacheco Bustios, a native of Locumba -actual Tacna-, and daughter of the also Creoles José Carlos Pacheco and Benavides, and María Nicolasa de Bustios y Palacios. This union had the following descendants: Blas Fernando de Lezo y Pacheco, first Marquis of Oviedo., Posthumous title inherited from his father and entitled to succession. Tomás de Lezo y Pacheco, Governor of Santa Cruz de la Sierra, and Ignacia Antonia de Lezo, married to the first Marquis de Tabalosos, also in succession. Her Excellency Mrs. Doña Josefa Pacheco was buried in the Convent of Santo Domingo, located in the street of the same name. As of this date, the descendants of Blas de Lezo disappeared from the port records.

However, although the feats of Blas de Lezo fall short of the greatest sailors in history, he is a virtually forgotten character. Currently, there is talk of a Spanish company that is preparing a documentary about his life and there are some streets with his name in Spain, including one in Madrid, but that is not enough. Blas de Lezo is, of course, a recognized hero in Cartagena de Indias, who pays homage in several ways: neighborhoods, avenues and squares commemorate him in their names; and his statue in front of the San Felipe bastion keeps the memory of the defender of his city alive among the people of Cartagena.

But after the English defeat in Cartagena in 1741 and the Franco-Spanish fleet in Trafalgar in 1805, the dominance of England and Spain in the New World colonies was destined to disappear. In this fight of crossed destinies between these two powers, only the continent's natives would benefit.

However, during the twentieth century, dark feelings were still numb there, incubating, until they were awakened once again by the unjust actions of the Americans who arrived at the Department of Chocó with two companies, one to extract gold and platinum and another to associate with Banana growers in the Urabá region and in other areas of Colombia.

But that was not all, the seeds of hatred and resentment promoted by privateers and merchants since colonial times and fueled by American greed, took root with drug trafficking born in the twentieth century, a business that gave more than gold, silver, platinum and bananas, with a more complex and efficient management. Eventually the drug traffickers would become the new privateers, they made mini submarines and equipped speedboats, bought airplanes and were willing to risk their lives, killing those who got in their way in order to take their products to North America to sell them there to the highest bidder. It was only necessary to sow coca plants or marijuana in small clearings scattered in the tropical forest and process them in hidden places under the forest cover. The next step was to export the results.

In order to control the outbreaks of 'illicit crops', the government then decided to appeal to the fumigation with glyphosate, a fateful chemical that once used killed not only such plants but also all others, thus addressing the richest planet's area in biodiversity. Certainly, a crime committed against humanity and disguised as legal and innocent. After the chemical spread, nothing grew again, the animals died for lack of food or were forced to migrate to other sites. Of that ecological disaster, very few found out and the native population was powerless to prevent it.

At this time, the descendants of the first Barnabas Abundá were hundreds that inhabited the two Colombian coasts., some no longer used the name and had forgotten where they came from, they only knew that their color testified that they were originally from Africa and made to endure the tropics' sun, in a land lost in the consciousness of its own people. A large piece of a homeland that had always turned its back on them, to that land with two seas and palm trees moved by the wind, large butterflies with blue wings and humpback whales, which deserved to be held high not only for their suffering and its history, but also for its richness, its beauty and the immense potential hidden in its entrails.

3

The clock of his death would be activated with the eclipse. With trembling wings, the butterfly marked the seconds, the minutes, the days that remained, like the ticking of the inexorable clock of life in its eternal advance. The whale for its part in its greatness contained all the hope of a world about to disappear forever. Barnabas did not suspect how close he was to losing everything. His wife neither. It is not that he cared to die, on the contrary, he looked at death as the only solution to its existence. She thought differently, she was afraid of it. Everything was written. She heard that those who escaped death, by a strange mockery of fate, sooner or later were with her in terrible circumstances. Death never forgave anyone no matter how many times people made fun of or hid from it. Fate dice were thrown on the cosmic hopscotch where they ultimately won. Death always triumphed, always ...

It was the morning of the eclipse when Barnabas met the whale. He never thought that on his return he would no longer have a wife or whom to tell what he had seen. A blow like a giant slap shattered his keel and fired him overboard. He had embarked at dawn, at dawn, but at that time, something strange had happened, the star had begun to hide behind the moon, like an omen and it was so dark, that Barnabas's hands were lost in the shadows. The gannets and seagulls had ducked their heads, sticking their beaks to their bodies and the giant blue-breasted cicadas had sung again.

His ship's sail did not even reflect the faded whiteness of a thousand suns, with a tattered cloth, spoiled by salt and the inclement rain of that place. He felt cold and suddenly, he heard a long moan, like that of a lover in heat when he climaxed with his beloved or the siren of a sinking ship, desperately seeking help. A thick fog began to come down from the mountains, which got into the sea and covered the trees with its mantle. The moan faded with the fog and its echo could be heard everywhere. Barnabas at that moment felt a chill and began to search the water for some piece of wood that could have been saved from the shipwreck. It was impossible to know where the coast was. The half bottle of rum with which he had breakfast, still burned his guts and felt like vomiting. Suddenly, a piece of candle that floated near him, became entangled in one of his legs. He hoped the mast of eaten wood would still be tied to her, like the soul of a dying man to his body. The mist was now so thick that he could not see the water or the color of his skin and again he heard a breath, and another and another. Barnabas felt the current dragging him. That sea was treacherous and he realized that he was adrift and did not know where he was going to stop. Not that he cared much, because the line that separated life from death was so thin, in those places, that sometimes it was better to die rather than live. At that moment, a strong wind began to blow and the mist showed the sun's rays escaping through the clouds as if a miracle were going to happen. That day, death would pass his scythe brushing it three times. If he was still alive, it was thanks to a piece of wood that had decided not to leave him, looking for him like a faithful dog and a whale that had frightened sharks. That morning, while he was drifting, death had forgiven him for dying shattered by a gas cylinder, which had been thrown into the hall where the villagers had taken refuge. A guerrilla group had decided to kill them all but failed. Two were saved that day, and one was Barnabas. He had gone fishing in the "Sonora" that had so many patches on the wood, as patches and seams had the fabric of the sail. When he arrived, three days later, the town was empty. The children did not play on the beach or in the sand square where the flag was raised on Sundays and the skinny dog who always went out to receive it and eat the leftovers of the egg muffins that Nila sometimes prepared for him, he did not see her either. The rain had extinguished any vestige of the fire that had consumed everything, even the foundations. All the people who had taken refuge in the "little school" had not been able to escape. It had been a massacre later called by newspapers the "Tragedy of Bojayá". Some murderous man, in an act of madness, had locked the doors from the outside, using an iron rod through the rings screwed to the wood, so that no one escaped and then he threw through a high window, the bomb made with a gas cylinder. The explosion that followed was so loud that it could be heard several miles around but was overshadowed by the waves' noise.

All had died asphyxiated and consumed by the fire and their bodies, not even the vultures could take advantage of the bodies, escaping to look for two dead cows that had perished drowned during the last rising of the gorge of San Onofre. It had been ten years since he finished his boat with a mast and a sail made with the cloth of the sacks of flour, which the 'gringos' left on the beach. When they did, it was to show how charitable they were. They had arrived there commanded by a sergeant who spoke in English and had made them understand that his purpose was to help them build a 'schoolhouse' that would also serve them as a church. No one ate the story, but the sergeant came with his soldiers in a gunboat that pointed his machine guns at the beach and had a letter from the government. In the distance the mother ship could be seen from where the gunboat had come from, waiting for its return a month later. The soldiers were divided into two groups, some were provided with weapons, maps, boxes and some rare devices that no one had ever seen and went into the jungle. Others were in charge of the construction of the school, which, without knowing it at that time, would all serve as a grave someday. When they finished, they raped two women and left two blue-eyed mulattoes born nine months later.

The moan was heard now in a different, deaf tone, like the wheeze of an injured animal, accompanied by a long breath and he could hear it by his side. Then he felt a fine, warm rain that fell on his face. Again, a blow, like that of a huge paddle lashing the sea hard, made him swallow water. This time the fog showed a gray lump, like a mountain floating near him. It was a humpback whale, which stopped there. He realized that perhaps it was looking for its son or both had suffered the misfortune of having fallen into the trap of some harpoon ship, of the many who fished illegally in those waters. He decided to swim in the direction where he was and ventured to touch her. He had nothing to lose and if he was going to die, he could at least remember, he had touched a whale. It was as lonely as he was and was also adrift, it singing weaker, still calling for life. When he felt the smooth animal's skin, he began to caress it and speak to it in his hoarse voice of rum drinker and a smoker of toasted tobacco in the flame of a candle. It was so wet on those coasts, that the custom was necessary, otherwise, they did not burn. "Look, he told the whale, don't worry, if we're going to die, it's better if we're together." The whale looked at him with the only eye with which it could see him, on the side of its head. At that moment, a giant-winged butterfly with blue wings that glowed with the sun, in a fog that was beginning to dissipate, went to perch on its hump and was saved from drowning. And so, Barnabas, the whale, and the butterfly drifted along the water.

Then he thought of Nila, the woman he found in Santa Marta, on the promenade, in front of the square, where she sold 'egg muffins', fried in reheated oil and covered with salt. She was a frank-faced mulatto, with a smile with white teeth like the shells of the sea and she sang while stirring her bowl with a ladle. She had spoken to him many times after their first meeting and had returned to that place every morning for breakfast, before continuing with his trade as a freighter in the port. In these meetings, he asked her many times to go live with him, to a paradise, on an unknown beach, bathed by waterfalls that descended from the mountains through a thick jungle and where she could sell her muffins as, those that sometimes she accommodated in a big plate over her head, announcing them when she walked and sung in the street.

On Sundays I saw her in Taganga, facing the sea, where she was going to sell her muffins to tourists and he also liked to go there. They started talking while eating a ceviche under an almond tree and each one talked about their dreams for a better future. He taught her how to play dominoes and he bet that sooner or later she would be his wife. At that time Nila was wearing old rubber sandals and the first gift that Barnabas had given her was a pair of canvas shoes that never fit her and she had to return them. But one day, Barnabas got tired of insisting, felt like traveling and left north and Nila never saw him again. She missed his company and his athlete's body lying on the sand and although until then they had never been together, she imagined what it would be like to do with such a black man. And while she kept selling her muffins and sometimes thought about him, Barnabas was going around the Sierra Nevada, in a journey that would last almost two years and that he never forgot. When he returned, one Sunday he looked for her in Taganga and managed to convince her to leave with him in search of lost paradises and their destinies would unite for a while and then take unexpected directions, with an even stranger ending than they could ever have imagined.

Thanks to a debt that was paid with a favor, Barnabas, had managed to get a captain to take them on a patrol boat that bordered the Caribbean Coast, then penetrate the Gulf of Urabá following the course of the Atrato River to "Vigía del Fuerte del Chocó". There they disembarked and followed the 'gold route', and after two weeks in the jungle, they arrived at Playa Huesos -Bone's Beach-, not far from "Nuquí". At that time, the sandals no longer existed and both were barefoot, but they didn't seem to care. In the backpack that Barnabas bought before embarking on the trip was all his luggage: two hammocks, a pita net, the muffin's frying pan, two shirts and an old pant, a razor, a machete, a string ball and two thin cloth dresses Nila owned, a box of cigars, two box of matches, one needle, two pounds of rice, two candles and a bottle of rum. They did not need much more, some of the town inhabitants had less

♣♣♣

The whale resolved again. The butterfly on its hump was still there, moving its blue wings like turquoise, drying them in the wind and orienting them to the sun. Barnabas remembered the black iguanas, which he had seen doing the same, when standing on the rocks, they all lined up, next to each other and remained motionless, heating their blood with the midday sun. Then he was hungry when he thought of the iguanas or the eggs' chain they laid and that Nila sometimes prepared for him and they were good for making love by accompanying them with a bottle of rum. When he thought of that, he felt his mouth dry with sea saltpeter. The coast was far away, his fingers wrinkled and numb and his eyes ached from the glare at the sun's reflections on the waves. He decided to swim with one arm, because the other was still clinging to the mast and bordering the whale's body to protect himself with its shadow, it was then when he saw it. A harpoon had penetrated the animal's body, to one side, under its fin and a piece of rope that dragged on the surface of the water hung from it. Barnabas began to caress the whale's skin while it was watching him with the eye on the other side of its head. For some reason, the animal sensed what the man was going to do and his hoarse voice seemed to reassure her. — Look—, he said again —, it may hurt, but sometimes some pain is necessary to continue living and thus appreciate life. Don't die yet, hold on a little longer ... and arming himself with courage, Barnabas dropped his piece of wood, took the rope, tied it to one of his arms without exerting any pressure on the harpoon and then leaned his feet against the whale's body and pulled with all his might towards him. The animal blew and sank, leaving a trail of blood in the water. Barnabas felt his body when he was dragged to the bottom of the sea by the weight of the harpoon, tied to his left arm and making a great effort, managed to free himself from the rope and get rid of drowning. That day, death had touched him with his scythe for the third time.

Exhausted, he managed to see the mast, thanks to the bluish reflections of the butterfly wings that had perched there and swam towards it. The outline of the sierra was outlined against the sky and there was a forest of coconut palms and a huge ceiba tree on which the vultures that were eating the two dead cows had stood. Two hours later, he released the mast and managed to reach the beach. The butterfly followed him and went to lose itself in the dense jungle. Crawling, he reached the palms' shadow and stood there. He took a knife from his pocket that was saved from the wreck and managed to extract water from a coconut and quench thirst and hunger by consuming its sweet white flesh. He remembered the stories his mother once read to him about people who fed on something similar that had come down from the sky and began to dream about the sand. He was alive, like the whale and the butterfly. The three of them had been saved! That night he slept there. It was still dark when the whale's breath woke him up. This time it sounded different; it was looking for him. He ran without fear and went into the sea and soon saw it. It was there, immense, bigger than his boat, and blood was not flowing from its side. The whale looked at him with its right eye. It had come to thank him for saving its life. The water was cold, then, it wheezed and threw a jet of water into the air and beating his tail hard, it submerged and never saw her again that day. That's life, he thought, today I'm here and not tomorrow, and he remembered the blue-winged butterfly and Nila's egg muffins.

When he arrived home two days later, he felt loneliness and that something happened. The townspeople had disappeared as if by charm. Suddenly he found the dog, his tail was between its legs, its ears bowed and it was thinner than usual and that was when he didn't see the school hall that sometimes served as a church. She thought the angels had taken it with everyone inside and deep down he was right. When he got there, his heart cringed as he walked through the rubble and felt the smell of scorched meat. The calcined skeletons scattered on the ground testified to the massacre that had taken place. Somewhere, he picked up a white shell necklace that he had given Nila on her birthday and remembered her smile ...Beyond, a huge, blue-winged butterfly had stood where the altar had been, flapping its wings and orienting them to the sun. That night, the jungle heard a long, hoarse groan that was repeated endlessly, it was the parting song of Barnabas. In the distance, a groan like his was returning to the beach, brought by the waves and the wind that begun to blow. When dawn broke, he entered the water and swam as far as the forces reached him. There was the whale, waiting for him, with a huge blue-winged butterfly standing on its hump and that was when he saw her dive into the sea and no one saw them again.

The afternoon when Nila left behind what was left of her life, she thought she had no husband and no one to complain about her misadventures. She never imagined that she would be a widow and that Barnabas would be killed for no reason, because he owed nothing to anyone, nor did he speak more than needed. She could not bury him, nor discover among the rubble, what his skeleton was. There were no people left in the town to help her and that is why she decided to go to the port and wait for the gunboat that passed through there and leave as far as she could. As a farewell, she returned the necklace of white shells he had given her, looked for the largest skeleton she could find and set it aside, in case her soul was hovering, at least to accompany him, while she could take revenge. Barnabas went fishing early and never arrived after ten. Later, the sea was curling and the return was difficult, with a wind against it coming down from the "Sierra de los Saltos". More than one had been lost and had never returned.

The coastal relief was rocky and there were several shrimp's species such as marmosets, but if the currents and the hours of fishing were known, the tiger and the coffee shrimp were obtained in the morning hours and the white and red a little later farther north. Making a courage display, Barnabas had ventured with his boat to fish prawns in deeper waters. What was best for him was to follow the gannets that were detected by the anchovy or tuna banks and was an expert in knowing the coastal corners, preferred by sea bass, catfish, red snappers, and the hiding places of the groupers. After arriving, he left the fish in the cooperative and went to the school to receive classes from the teacher sent by the government less than three months ago. It was the best he could do. Very soon they would have to leave the town, since the guerrillas had threatened them since the captain had arrived with his soldiers and he thought it was better to instruct himself in case they had to leave. Not that he knew where to go. He had lived so long near the sea that he was not interested in going to die of the cold on some mountain inland. Many times, he thought he was better off dead than displaced, but Nila thought otherwise and that with her muffins, they would never lack anything. She would put a business in any corner where death was not around and Barnabas could help her with anything and learn something of the trade. It didn't seem like such a bad idea.

The place had become a dangerous place since a captain had settled on the other side of the river, in Playa Huesos -Bones Beach-, where sometimes humpback whales were going to die, leaving their skeletons and huge bones bleached by the sun, scattered on the sand, in a final act of purification, reminiscent of the Flood and the ribs of Noah's Ark. When they arrived, with songs that nobody understood, in their notes they could hear nostalgia and a call of sadness. They got into the cove, at the mouth of the river and died there. No one knew why. The village cemetery was a little higher, in a jungle clearing, from where the sea could be seen. The dead were buried in a hole in the sand, as there was no money for a drawer, nor a carpenter to make one. The custom was to put plastic flowers on top of each grave that shone with the sun, did not wilt and did not serve as food for ants. Each dead person had that special mark that way. Some made bouquets of red tulips and others of yellow roses that did not occur in that place. The children were given white lilacs and colored lilies mixed with lilies of Saint Joseph. The captain had ordered the soldiers to make him a table with a bone of a vertebra and to use some of the ribs for a rocking chair. Nila that day had seen them cutting them with a saw. She was bathing with her yellow flower dress glued to her body, in the river of crystalline waters, a little above the post established by the military, when two shots rang out and then she heard a few clicks between the branches and saw when a howler red hair monkey, slipped off a huge tree and fell like a bundle against the floor. It was the captain's lunch. She hid behind a log that was dragged there by the last crescent and waited. The silence had eaten the jungle with the shots and the noise and shrieks of hundreds of birds and other monkeys had been left behind. The soldiers' voices were heard between the thicket and a shout when someone told the others:

—Here it is, I found it, is still alive, it is better to finish it off with a knife, because the captain does not like to spend more bullets! She felt a chill. The animal was lying on the ground and looked at the soldiers with a grimace of pain but without uttering any howling. His black eyes, like two glass spheres, did not contain any expression of hate and rather implored compassion. She decided to get out of the water and face the soldiers:

—Wait—! she shouted—, don't kill it! Let it live! I have two big crayfish and a lobster and I can exchange them for it. What do you say?

The soldiers felt bewildered to see the mulatto. The one who went ahead answered:

— And what are we going to tell the captain? He heard the two shots...

—Tell him the truth, if you want, I go with you, and if he agrees, I can cook the lobster and also the crayfish. They are fresh, I caught them early this morning.

— And what do we do with the monkey meanwhile?

—Nothing, leave it where it is, I'll come later for it. It seems that one of the bullets pierced its shoulder and went to the other side and the wound is clean. The other doesn't seem to have touched it.

And while Nila was explaining her business to the captain, it was when the explosion was felt. The whole forest shook with it and then a black smoke could be seen the other side of the river, next to the jungle. The soldiers ran in all directions and shouts were heard through the thicket. Then the firing of the machine guns could be heard not far from where the animal had been. Nila instead ran in the direction of the smoke, which came from the town corner, where the "little school" was, she was horrified by what she saw. Six columns of black smoke rose to the sky, scaping the room's high windows and a few moments later, the flames licked the treetops, forming fantastic figures. She ran desperate to open the door and found it closed, with a rod pierced between two rings and bent in such a way that she could do nothing. Inside she seemed to hear screams of pain and then only the crackling of the flames that rose to heaven in a sacrificial offering. The wooden structure was quickly consumed by fire and the smell of charred wood and scorched flesh could be felt everywhere when it mixed with the mist that came down from the mountains and covered the beach with its mantle.

4

That morning, without thinking about it, Barnabas decided to return by the same road where he had come and start again in Santa Marta, in the same place where met Nila. He had nothing on him except for a knife in his pocket and his double-edged machete. The platter for accommodating the muffins as well as the backpack and the sardine box where they kept their savings, he did not see them and thought that the guerrillas had stolen them. The trip through the jungle trails would take several days and now everything seemed different. The rage went inside and with each step he took, he buried her a little more.

He did not release a tear, not because he had not loved Nila, but because man did not cry and he was one of those. That was how his mother had taught him:

—"Eat your tears—, she said—, crying is useless, it does not take away your hunger, sadness, or give you more money—. He had never cried and that was why he had his soul with a stiffer callus than the soles of his feet. That night, he heard voices in the jungle. There were three men, they were celebrating and they had killed a 'pajuil' -wild turkey-. They were roasting it on top of a bonfire and had scarcely removed its feathers. One of them commented between laughter, how the bodies had flown with the gas cylinder and the one in front answered him that he was satisfied that he had complied with the 'Boss' ...

—Now—, he said—, they will give me the command of a front for me alone and you'll see ... Barnabas first froze when he remembered Nila and then felt his head boil. A wave of anger rose from his feet, burning his insides in his path. With his machete in his hand and the speed of a panther in the shadow, he pounced on the three men. To the one who was laughing, his head rolled down the hill with his smile on and the one in front of him cut off a hand that jumped through the air and went to fall at the stake. When he looked for the third one, he no longer saw him, he had fled down the mountain and left his weapon behind him. The man implored him not to kill him, but Barnabas thought again of Nila and without saying a word, pierced his heart. Then he checked the dead and the headless man, he was able to take off some boots that served him. He felt no remorse. On the contrary, he was relieved to have avenged Nila and the dead of his people. In one of the campaign backpacks he found money, a gas lighter, three cans of sausages, two of sardines, a flashlight, a cotton blanket and a rubber poncho to protect him from the rain. In the other there was also money, two candles, three tobaccos, two cans of ham and two of peach, a small pan and a bottle of brandy. Of the dead he also obtained two water bottles, a mountain knife, a compass, a map and a clock. The submachine guns, as he didn't know how to use them, decided to leave them there with another machete he didn't need, his two-edged was enough. He put out the fire and continued along the coast at the height of where he was, while the dead had begun to be eaten by red ants and flies once they smelled blood.

He remembered his own village once more. Everything had been abandoned and life was gone forever. He walked through the rubble where the church had been, but the rain had taken the ashes and turned them into mud and he remembered Nila and the white shell necklace he gave her.

At the edge of a river he found an abandoned raft stranded on a black sandbar, with a long paddle, and a fishing line, because in those waters the catfish abounded. Under the bar he saw two large sieves to look for nuggets of gold and platinum straining the sand, and a leather bag containing hooks and two rusty coins. He pushed the raft, mounted on it and let it go with the flow. It was raining and it would be a couple of days before he could get to the Atrato and from there, a couple of weeks if I wanted to find the sea. He had everything he needed, except a woman, but he preferred not to look for one in those places. He had a fresh memory of the men he had killed and didn't know if others were looking for him. One had escaped and had seen him and the jungle and rivers had ears that he knew well. That night he would make a stop before the mouth of the Atrato, the great river that the government had planned to turn into a canal to replace that of Panama, but things had never progressed and fortunately everything remained the same. Progress, he thought, only served so that the rich had more money and the poor had nothing.

He tied the raft on a dark shore, and got into a cedars and palms' forest, crowned by giant ceibas that choose that place to seeking sunlight. Lianas and mold-filled vines hung everywhere like a giant's beard and spider monkeys and insects made a deafening noise. He set fire to some sticks he found dry under a rock and walked through his life in the shadows of his memory, suddenly the jungle was silent in a quiet moment and then it was the excitement. The macaws woke up and began to fly blindly, in all directions. He felt a presence but could not see anything, then a hoarse growl and then again silence. This time he felt the presence near him, he could almost touch it with his breath. Suddenly he saw the red eyes of an animal with the flames of the bonfire, like lightning, jumped to the side and machete in hand faced him. The jaguar did not know how to react and his instinct advised him that it was better to leave that black body that moved through the shadows, with reflections of fire glued to his skin.

At dawn he caught a catfish, roasted it over low heat and ate breakfast. He continued his journey along the river until he reached the Atrato's mouth and docked in front of "Vigia del Fuerte". He had been there before when he arrived with Nila on his way to the Pacific coast and remembered with gratitude the patrol boat's captain that took them to that place, on a hundred of kilometers' journey that did not cost them a single cent.'

The captain told them that the amount of gold that came out of the Atrato was such, that three hundred years ago, a Scottish corsair managed to board a Spanish galleon in whose wineries he found 300 pounds of that metal that were destined for Spain, a tax that the mine owners had to pay tribute to the king and stole them. But history repeats itself and what he never imagined is that the same fort and 'the gold route' were helped to build by one of their ancestors, the first one arrived at the Atrato and the Chocó 500 years before. Then Barnabas thought of the corsair's greed, Lina and felt hunger and a rage in the soul that he could not overcome. When he saw the fort ruins and the cobbled road that reached the shore, he paddled there and landed. He sat under a Ceiba and for the first time in his life cried watching the river run. In his memory the memories swirled again and he felt guilty of having taken Nila along the path of death, in search of lost paradises. Not that he was afraid of death, he had seen her closely so many times that he was convinced it was the soul's best friend. He also thought that death was afraid of him and that was why he had dodged it so many times. The captain's book said that the fort's ruins were what remained of past glories, when the Spaniards decided to protect the ports that were on the river and on a bend they raised a fort, where they placed six cannons brought from Spain, at the mouth of the Bojayá and that they called it Watchman of the Fort of Bojayá. Two of the cannons could still be seen with their rust puff lying on a wall. The road that led from the fort to the Pacific was paved in long stretches with the sweat and tears of blacks brought from Africa to extract gold and platinum from alluvium and although it was used for almost three centuries, with the fall of the colonial government, the fort and the road were abandoned, only the guerrillas had discovered their strategic importance and were mobilizing there. All the inhabitants of the area dreamed for centuries with a path to the sea, but in those places, the government rarely carried out its promises. The lonely jungle in its naive beauty and splendor, devoured everything covering it with its mantle, while its inhabitants fought against injustice and for their livelihood under an inclement rain that never stopped.

No one was interested in a black man traveling alone downstream on a raft and no one stopped him. The jungle or the cliffs on the sides of the river did not let him see beyond and the Atrato was wide enough for him to feel safe. He took out the map he had taken from the guerrilla and saw that Quibdó had remained upriver and that the next large hamlet would be Opogodó.

He thought of stopping there if he saw it. Along, several fishing canoes passed him, but he was so tired that he fell asleep on the raft and did not see them. When the fishermen saw him lying on it, they thought that there was another dead person, of the many they saw on their trip to the sea. The bodies almost never arrived complete and were eaten by vultures, piranhas or other larger fish. In that jungle, nothing was wasted and everything was recycled. Suddenly he felt a blow and jumped up. He had run aground on the left bank and in the distance, he saw two lights and decided to approach them. He walked to a hamlet whose owner was dedicated to washing the sands of the banks with sieves like his own. If someone was lucky and found gold or platinum, he kept it in a little bag, then sold it to the Lebanese or the Turks who traveled the river. The merchants had discovered that this system was cheaper and had no social benefits and thus exploited blacks for decades.

But before the blacks, it was the Indians who had suffered the inclemency of the greed pendulum. As of December 25, 1510, one year after San Sebastián was founded, on the other side of the gulf and looking for a place where the Indians were supposedly less aggressive, "Santa María la Antigua del Darién" was founded, located in the middle of the jungle , about five kilometers from the shore of the Gulf of Urabá, near the border with Panama. Since then, the Indians had been brutally massacred by the hard hand of the conquerors. Its Founder Martín Fernández de Enciso proclaimed laws so unfair, that his same partners rebelled against him. He even prohibited any treatment between Spaniards and Indians, which had to do with gold and of which he had not been previously informed, executing whoever did not fulfill his orders.

His greed had no limits, wanting absolute control of all the wealth there was and his name went down in history, having been deposed from his self-proclaimed position of governor, like that of a man covered by the shadow of cruelty and greed. The name of the city was due to the suggestion made by Vasco Núñez de Balboa, the discoverer of the Pacific three years later, of fulfilling a promise made to the Virgin, if they managed to defeat the Indians who presented a brave and just defense of its territory, commanded by the chief Arién. Hence the name Darien. Balboa himself was responsible for deposing and returning Fernández de Enciso to Spain, but this was a big mistake. His resentment could more than his nobility and succeeded in falsifying the King's opinion unfavorably about the great conqueror. In return, they sent an old man with a double soul, envious and of little merit, Don Pedro Arias Dávila, known as 'Pedrarias'.

Upon his return from the Pacific, Balboa was carrying 40,000 pesos in gold and more pearls than he could ever dream of. After sending to the Spanish Crown 20 percent of the gold, according to the laws of the conquest, the rest was distributed among his men, but the fact is that there were so many pearls, that he managed to send the King 250 kilos of the finest.

Some curious mind in 1908 came to value those pearls at more than nine million US dollars. More than a third of what the United States paid Colombia for Panama. But that gesture would not help much to Balboa, who was soon separated from his wife, the beautiful Anna Yansi, daughter of Chief Careta, whom Balboa had defeated about sixty miles from there, in the middle of the jungle, making him a prisoner along with his whole family, achieving his subsequent conversion in a noble and persuasive way. When the chief offered his concubine's daughter, in a gesture of good will, Balboa refused to do so by making him his wife.

Forced by 'Pedrarias', to marry his own daughter, Balboa was forced to put Anna Yansi aside. However, the marriage was never consumed. The pendulum of envy had swung and this time it was on the side of betrayal.

From 1514 the advance of Santa María la Antigua del Darién was notorious. One hundred houses were built, a cathedral, the church of San Sebastián, the Foundry House, the convent of San Francisco, and a hospital. An immense black, leader of one of the slave gangs helped in its construction. It was Barnabas Abundá, one of the distant ancestors of Barnabas. The inhospitable climate where mosquitoes and diseases such as malaria, dengue and dysentery abounded, as well as the founding of Panama City, led to its abandonment five years later. The only testimony that remained as a memory of its existence and that is still kept in a museum, were a cannon, nails and rusty ironworks, some dishes made in Spain and some pieces of indigenous pottery. The rest was swallowed by the jungle and the hand of man. The name of what was one of the first cities founded in America is scarcely remembered today. But something would not die and those were the descendants of the black slaves who survived the inclemency, injustice and battles that came with the centuries.

Pedrarias, in a fatherly tone, wrote a letter to Balboa to tell him that his daughter was waiting for him and came to convince Francisco Pizarro himself to cross him on the road, making him his prisoner and so it was. After a wicked trial in which Balboa was denied all right of petition and long enough to defend himself against the false arguments with which he was accused, he was only granted to confess his sins with a Benedictine and the day after he arrived was beheaded and his head put in a pike in the middle of the square for everyone's lesson. And so, the Isthmus claimed its most famous victim, the greatest of all the conquerors of the New World and the discoverer of the great sea on St. Michael's Day. If Balboa had not died, very different would have been the conquest of the Maya who would have fallen into the hands of the treacherous, bloodthirsty, and great conqueror Hernán Cortés, Marqués de Oaxaca.

But it's as if all those who had to go through there had fallen from the curse of the greed demon. Many of the Spanish ships loaded with gold and pearls sank with their treasures, due to the storms and the 'teredo' worms, some tropical molluscs as harmful as the conquerors themselves, showing a bulging head with a lollipop in front and a tail Forked with two blades capable of trespassing the hardest wood, eating it. That had been the reason for the brigs to line their keels with metal hulls and to the wood varnish it with pitch, but despite this, given the necessary time, the worms that grew up to 60 centimeters, and were able to end any ship.

Everyone wanted a piece of Chocó's wealth. Not only the Spaniards in ancient times had passed through there but also the Germans, the French and the 'gringos' in recent times and none had reported a penny to the region or the country. The unfair American company Chocó-Pacífico with all its subsidiaries had extracted thousands of pounds of gold, silver, and platinum with the sweat of blacks and had only left them poverty and bastard children. Platinum had been used as currency in Condoto, on the banks of that river, in the highlands of San Juan and its exploitation, lasted until 1980. In 1925, more foreigners arrived and that was when the Turks, the Germans and the Lebanese made their august. How much foreign companies obtained since the Chocó-Pacific set up a power plant in

1916, it was never known. And then, when navigating that river and walking through these jungles, it was easy to understand the foreigners' greed and the naivety of their natives, and how the centuries like a thick crust, had fermented pus underneath of hatred and resentment, but somehow, that land was waking up in spite of itself, like a sleeping giant, after its lethargy. If the 'teredo' worms had been the terror of any flag navigators in the past, certain species had begun to reveal themselves. It was as if the 'Jaibaná's curse of the Emberá Catíos' tribe had been heard:

In recent times a singular fact never seen before. Thousands of bats were threatening the 16,000 inhabitants of Condoto, in the south of Chocó. The band of vampires only fed on human blood and had established a fence around the population that had already been several weeks suffering from its attacks. Half a hundred people had been bitten and their blood sucked as in a strange ritual of the guardian spirits that the Indians invoked in the upper Bojayá River. It was as if the souls of those who were cremated within the church, had decided to escape in order to take revenge on all the inhabitants of the region. So far, no cases of rabies had been recorded, but that would not take long to occur. The missionaries spoke that it was one of the apocalyptic plagues announced for thousands of years and that the morning when the eclipse happened was the harbinger of the announced end. Spokesmen of the San José de Condoto hospital, on the other hand, affirmed that this population was on the migratory route, which the animals used for millennia. For more than a year, they had increased their numbers and consolidated their forces, beginning to move from Lower Baudó to the southwest of the state. The lack of electricity for more than three months had also helped their proliferation, as they were darkness' lovers and acted on it without detection.

No one had been able to sleep for a single night, for terror had taken hold of everyone and the flutter could be heard in the shadows after six o'clock, which was the time the vampires came out to feed. When they left, the sky was dyed black with flocks of animals that flew in all directions and it was not ruled out that the vampires would soon move to other neighboring places along the river.

One of the causes of the massive arrival of these flying mammals was the geographical location of Condoto in the San Juan river basin and although the authorities tried to prevent the animals from biting more people, capturing them or spreading poisons that went from the 'curare' al 'pakurú-niaara', so that they would kill each other by licking among themselves, they had not been more successful. However, control work had been complicated by the growing mining activity in the extraction of gold and platinum and by the darkness prevailing in the area due to the blasting of energy towers by the guerrillas and the lightning and storms that caused Continuous electrical failures.

The mining that was previously artisanal deteriorated the environment due to the intense deforestation and the use of backhoes, which had affected the decrease of animals such as cows and pigs that served as food for the bats, forcing them to bite the humans. But the worst was the government's decision to deforest national parks with 'glyphosate', a high-potency and toxicity herbicide that was killing entire ecosystems. It was certainly a crime, not only against the region, but against humanity. Its pretext was that with it the hidden fields of poppy or marijuana were controlled, but the consequences were not measured. The land was barren for years, insects disappeared and birds, mammals and reptiles of all kinds lost their livelihoods and were doomed to emigrate to other sites or to die. All this to please a group of national and foreign legislators who sought, not the extinction of the drug, but the monopoly of their cultivation or the sale of their chemicals, with huge profits.

Neither the measures nor the rabies vaccines had been able to put a stop to that plague of apocalyptic nature, which had been taught first with the children, these being the most defenseless. This was not the first time that the inhabitants of Chocó had to move due to their misfortunes or extreme misery.

Many of Choco's inhabitants, due to poverty, had emigrated to the north and crossed the border with Panama. At the beginning of the last century, Chocó had lost two thirds of its people. The wealth of Panama was legendary since its foundation in 1518 by

Pedrarias and in 1670 it had reached the peak of its splendor, as it was the crossing point between Spain and Peru, to the south, and Veracruz and down California to the north, passing through there almost all the riches of the new world and becoming the new gold route. And it was then, during the reign of Charles II of England, in the last quarter of a century, that piracy had also reached its climax. Spain by then, had lost 60 million crowns, a calculation that only covered the destruction of towns and cities, without the loss of more than 250 merchant ships and frigates. It was, in fact, the balance of piracy sponsored from Jamaica, an island under the protection of the English, who since then, lived peacefully from plantations and smuggling. When, in 1671, the English privateer Henry Morgan put siege to Panama City, plundering it, setting it on fire and raping its women, he obtained a booty that he transported using more than four hundred horses. In recent times, it was easy to find the surname Henry or Morgan in any telephone directory in Panama, which the women had given their offspring born five or six generations before, when not knowing the name of the rapist, they had adopted that of the privateer.

In response to these acts of pillage and vandalism, the Spaniards built a port in Bahía Cupica in the northern part of the Chocó's coast and opened the gold route between the Pacific and the Bojayá's river mouth over the Atrato, continuing it inland by Antioquia and Citará, fortifying the banks of the great river, with canyons that soon succumbed to the humidity and served more to frighten people than anything else.

But people keep memory not only of the bad but also of the good and if Panama's wealth had been legendary, its trade as well. From time immemorial, indigenous cultures took advantage of its wealth and crossed from one side of the continent to the other. In recent times, peasants filled their insecure barges with up to five tons of tagua wood and carried it there, but in return they received a kerosene lamp, a small change of clothes, a fuel bottle and if they were lucky, an ordinary perfume for women, and in more current times, sometimes not even the fuel to return, if the barge was propelled by an old 'Johnson'.

In a guerrilla newspaper, was announced that the 'gringos' latest invention was called TLC - Free Trade Agreement - and that this was a treaty to steal what was left of the wealth of a country. Not only gold, silver and platinum. Nothing would be saved and from now on, everything would belong to them with a government signature. The newspaper said also they had stolen Panama in the same way, but this time, their greed had reached the limit and with the story of globalization everything was theirs. They had discovered that it was easier to loot with a treaty and that was the cheapest way to conquer, without even having to fire a bullet. And so, without anyone noticing, what interested them most was that countries exterminate each other while they sold their weapons, their helicopters and their war debris and when there was someone who had the courage to denounce them, they accused him of drug trafficker or destabilizing the hemisphere. The newspaper also said that their most recent advances proved they wanted to "buy" Greenland with treacherous arguments which were soon discarded by the Danish government.

Then he remembered the men who had come to build the 'little school' and those who had gone into the jungle with boxes and strange devices and realized that what they were looking for were samples of plants and medicinal remedies that were cultivated in the villages' roofs for centuries and although he did not know it, with millenary roots and remedies that could be found in the Inca empire. He managed to think that they would soon be selling them in pharmacies, with a stamp that would say 'Packaged in the USA' and that in order to cure arthritis or gas gangrene users would have to pay exorbitant amounts in dollars and that no one would have the right to cultivate and exploit what they thought was theirs, without asking for their permission. That was the reason why the guerrillas with their promises, truths and lies had managed to set foot there, but that would not last long, their atrocities cried to heaven and men like Barnabas, they were everywhere, willing to exterminate them at any cost. But if the guerrillas had arrived, the paramilitaries had been sowing terror and anxiety, displacing the peasant communities of the Salaquí, Truandó and Domingodó basins, for economic interests using the sophistry of chasing the guerrillas.

On the other hand, the pendulum of greed had swung again on the side of terror. The guerrillas were generating fear and pressuring indigenous communities to lock themselves up and disappear in the jungle in subhuman conditions. Of the fifteen thousand who lived in Chocó, no one knew how many were left after being besieged by hunger and disease. The civil presence of the State was scarce and inefficient, allowing a vacuum that the groups tried to fill outside the law, with the only argument that they had the force of arms. A clear response was necessary to the serious humanitarian crisis that the indigenous, black and mestizo peasants of the Lower Atrato were suffering, with an uprooting so deep that it could lead to the final dispossession of their territory. Perhaps the ideas of federalism that had begun to emerge in the mid-19th century would have produced better results than the centralism that took place, since at least the inhabitants of the region would have known what to expect, without expecting anything from a central government that it had turned its back for hundred of years.

It was very hot and the humidity exaggerated it even more. Barnabas arrived at a group of lakeside dwellings held on sticks and that didn't seem to surprise him after having lived in the swamp when he was younger. They were safer and in case of a flood of the river, the water rose almost three meters, flooding several kilometers on the sides of the banks and that gave the villagers time to prepare and save their lives. The river was so deep, that ships of the great draft could enter sailing from the sea four hundred kilometers, without finding any obstacle and from there to its origins, it would still travel one hundred and sixty kilometers, in the middle of the natural wealth, splendor, and the most complex biodiversity in the world.

The noise was the only common binder in an America divided by the useless or powerless rulers' egolatries to tame those tropics, being more concerned with themselves and how the future would receive their names than to build a better world. Some had been lost in their own labyrinths, copying Bolivar, Castro, San Martin or Perón. It would have been easier if they had followed the example of the 'arrieras ants' or the Brazilian 'marabunta', all working for a common good, but neither language, poverty, or hunger had been able to unite people or countries in that necessary destiny. And that fight of crossed destinies was the one that had the continent divided. Those from the north with a 'manifest destiny' and those from the south with an 'uncertain destiny'.

5

At the beginning of the 19th century, privateers continued to make their own and the seas were unsafe places, where terrorists and looters of all kinds continued to rage against the schooners and Spanish ships. The greed for gold and silver of Chocó had remained in force for centuries, as it was its territory one of the first producers of gold and platinum in the world. The same happened with the silver mines of Bolivia and Peru, which were also legendary. When Manuel Mallo, a good-natured clown born in Popayan, adventurous, friendly and bold, had emigrated to Spain in search of fortune, it was after having tempted luck looking for how to make deals with Chocó's gold between Spaniards and Creoles, Nobody knows how much he got, but what it was true, is that he realized from the beginning, the difficulties and dangers that entailed and being a person of practical nature and good living, had decided to look for gold elsewhere.

Upon arriving in Madrid, he understood from the outset the promiscuous character of the Queen and decided to take from her all the benefits he could. He entered the guard's body and was soon noticed by María Luisa. Her husband King Charles IV never found out, as often happens in these cases, and if something suspected, she preferred to leave things like that. The Queen's bad breath was notorious and it was a relief to be away from her. She had begun to gain weight in an excessive way and her skin had cracked, taking a morbid and yellowish tone as a result of a disease that led to premature aging. Little by little, she began to lose all her teeth and her carnal appetites gave free rein to the unsatisfied and frustrated woman inside. Not even the guards of his regiment were saved from her voracity. Unable to help the Monarchs in the problems of the State, as Manuel Godoy, the queen's lover before him, Mallo preferred to dazzle the sovereign with his physical attractions.

Poor Maria Luisa she had been losing her charms and was not a difficult prey for an ambitious man like Mallo. Thus, when Godoy prevailed in the councils of Government, Mallo triumphed in the Queen's rooms. While Godoy went down in history, Mallo remained as an upstart and simple figurant, as a simple Queen's whim, as many others had been. But none of that seemed to bother Godoy, who despite the distaste he felt for the clown, saw him as a relief to his duties and obligations born from his own instincts and the insatiable Maria Luisa's appetite. Spain was bleeding slowly at the time and in spite of everything, the luxury and decay of the court was remarkable, in violent contrast with the naivety and misery of some of its overseas territories. If the Battle of Trafalgar and the English privateers had reduced it in their defense capacity, seizing their trade routes, sinking hundreds of ships and schooners, the French would bite a piece of land whenever they could. The King, besides being stupid, was regarded as an "enlightened despot," a faithful copy of the bad customs inherited from France.

Meanwhile, the promiscuity of the shameful Queen, was working her way and would go down in history. The Russian Ambassador in Madrid described her government as follows: "… repeated deliveries, indispositions, and, perhaps, a germ of hereditary disease had withered it completely:

the yellow complexion dye and the loss of the teeth were a fatal blow for her beauty. "Napoleon had decided to step on Spain with his boot and had succeeded. The executions to overshadow the rebellion of May 1, 1808 in Madrid, were recorded in the blood that flowed from Goya's brush. In the midst of this disruption, the American colonies began to feel oppressed by the rulers' hard hands and secret outbreaks of discontent were taking root and germinating in all media and in all places. The ground of the uprising that was to come had been slowly paid, where the Spaniards with their foolish and raised viceroys were stirring that broth of hatred. While it was true that the indignation of the Creoles was great when they learned of the invasion of the three thousand soldiers that Napoleon had sent to Spain, his concern was also great. They gladly swore their obedience to Ferdinand VII, son of King Carlos, when he fled to Bayonne with his shameless

Queen. Obsessive in her passion, María Luisa, tired of all the abuses, made Mallo an object of her morbidity. In order to have him close and fully available to her whims, she filled him with honors, privileges and gifts and installed him in a mansion near the Palace. Everyone noticed that something was happening with Mallo and everyone realized what was behind. Soon the courtiers began to make jokes and conjectures and played riddles. Some out of envy and others out of deep contempt for the low passions he embodied, were closing the circle of his enemies like a rope around his neck.

Soon, he found himself alone in court meetings and many stopped inviting or visiting him. Despite his power, he was forced to look for Americans living in Madrid, including some who were not even to his liking, meanwhile, Godoy did what he could in his position as Prime Minister of the Kingdom to save Spain from his descent as a world power, because it had become the 'shell of the pudridero -the shell of rotting-', just like the one that accommodated the body of the deceased kings. It was at that time, after the eclipse, that María Luisa had heard from Mallo himself, as the last convoy with several schooners escorted by two frigates, had never reached port. When she heard the news, she became enraged and managed to say that it would have been better if Spain had never had anything to do with those wild territories of the New World, because in some way, they were to blame because their wealth had awakened the greed of the privateers and the whole world. She managed to think about how many lovers she could have bought with the gold that had been lost. She had interpreted the eclipse as an omen to her glory and that of Spain and Manuel Mallo as a sinister halo to her own. From that moment, his decline was very rapid, to the point of having to hide to save his own life.

Such was the atmosphere of the kingdom when a young man who was predestined to liberate the colonies, having arrived at the port of Santoña in Santander and having spent all his resources, arrived in Madrid. After having left his bags at the post office, he went to his uncle Esteban's house who had been one of the guests to enjoy Mallo's residence and there he was greeted with affection and joy by whoever saw him, the son I wish I had to accompany him in his old age. When he left the port of La Guaira towards Spain in 1799, in the San Ildefonso, which had joined a convoy in Veracruz, escorted by war frigates to avoid the attacks of pirates. The orgies of the young Caraqueño of nineteen years, in the Hacienda San Mateo, had become legendary and traveled with him, kept in his mind and in his soul like fierce animals willing to escape. His first love disappointment had suffered when he had reached the rank of Deputy Battalion of

Disciplined Militias of the Aragua Valley a year ago. What he thought could have been a true love, was nothing more than a conflictive and capricious relationship with a Creole, daughter of a rich landowner and a mulatto, whose mother had emigrated from Chocó to Panama and from there had passed to the Guaira. That was perhaps his best contact with that forgotten land and that left a scratch on his soul. Of that love he only had frustration and a thorn in his heart that was going to burn for some time.

The voluptuous body of the Creole, with her aromas and its fiery force of mysterious jungles, had been impregnated in every corner of his skin and carved his memory. He had reached the battalion, hoping his uncles could take him away from his life of dissolute pleasures that seemed to never quench his appetite and tame a bit of his wayward, stubborn and willful spirit. A spirit born of an irreparable family loss, which showed the lack of affection and tenderness of a mother. He had been orphaned as a child and nothing, and no one could ever replace the void left by his parents. Perhaps the glory that at that time, neither knew nor intuited, would be the only one able to offer any means of comfort in the years to come.

Like any young man, Don Simón was tempted by the decay that surrounded him and enthralled by the nakedness of the courtesans showing their white and trembling flesh as vulnerable doves. In Madrid, he always took part in the parties and orgies to which he was invited by Mallo or by his uncle Esteban and forgot for some time his teachings and the austerity with which he had been educated. With Mallo, he soon met Queen Maria Luisa and had access to the court and her courtesans and her life began to take place in a comfortable environment, worthy of a marquis. He actively participated in deer and wild boar hunts in the morning hours and in the evenings in meetings, dances, parties and romantic getaways with those who surrendered to his facade or his verb. If on the one hand that was one of the faces of the coin it showed, the other was less favorable. Soon his finances were reduced to almost nothing and he was forced to resort to loans in order to maintain appearances and in the end his own subsistence. The products that exported his farms in Venezuela, arrived in Madrid with delays of many months and made his life in that place very difficult. He was not alone in this, for many Americans depended on convoys that were held first twice a year, escorted by war frigates and then only once. The attacks of the ships of the English pirates or sometimes the French had diminished the defensive force of Spain and its commerce with the colonies.

But what happened to all the gold that Spain extracted from its colonies for more than three centuries? Nobody knows it for sure. Of the many tons that were transported by the ships and arrived safely, there remain as impressive memory of magnificence two gigantic guards of solid gold, carefully carved and considered the largest in the world, the largest in Seville and the second in Toledo. The rest changed hands with wars and revolutions.

A forced trip to Bilbao had given Don Simon part of the hope. He was fleeing a cholera outburst, when passing through the Puerta de Toledo -Toledo's Door-, a platoon ordered him to stop in order to requisition him. His wounded pride and explosive temperament prompted him to work and clear the road with cuts and commanders, thinking that he was being persecuted by Godoy's troops who followed all the friends loyal to Mallo, who by then had fallen out of favor. But on the other hand, this was the perfect pretext to go in search of Maria Teresa, the daughter of Don

Bernardo who was at that time in Bilbao and had met her at the house of the Marquis de Ustariz. However, he did not find his lover. They had crossed the road, the one going and she back home in Madrid.

After a while in Bilbao, he got tired of the place and began to move along the coast, visiting Santillana del Mar, where illustrious vacationers such as King Alfonso X the Wise, almost seven hundred years before, had had a house to escape the inclement weather of Madrid's winters, with a lover who had given him ten children, being able to observe the stars better from there, while thinking about composing songs to the Virgin. In the north, Don Simon had tasted the delights of seafood and fish and had discovered the bottles of French wines that came through Bordeaux. Soon the wine of numbered bottles began to be scarce and the women who sometimes frequented abandoned him when they noticed his lack of resources. When he arrived in Madrid again, he did not wait any longer and dressed in a long light green coat, open in the back, letting him see the lace of his shirt and the buttons of his vest adorned with diamonds and a light brown beaker made in England, went to visit the lover of his dreams and the only one he would ever marry. Her father agreed to the marriage immediately, after thinking about it during his trip to Bilbao, where he had taken his daughter to distract her from the fierceness and verbosity of the Don Simón.

And it was thanks to this situation of economic narrowness produced by the corsairs' attacks on the Spanish schooners, the ideas sown by the encyclopedists of the French Revolution, his wife's death and the injustices that were being perpetrated in the colonies against its inhabitants, that the future hero had decided to return. And that had been later one of the rays of hope for the inhabitants of the

Chocó region, who tired of their vile exploitation for centuries and after several attempts of revolts and uprisings, soon adhered to the cause of freedom. However, their situation did not change substantially and the injustices continued to be perpetuated to this day. The place left by the Spaniards was soon occupied by other foreigners who sowed fear, injustice, disappointment, sadness, and resentment, incubating them again as a poison in the souls of their inhabitants.

And yet, from that ungrateful land, illustrious men, including three Colombian presidents, who later rendered great services to the republic, such as Don Manuel María Mallarino, who had achieved a treaty with the US in 1846, leaving an inheritance which allowed their countrymen, free navigation on the Isthmus, especially benefiting the inhabitants of Chocó. His widow, Mrs. Mercedes Cabal Borrero, had been the heroine personified by the famous 'María' from the novel by Jorge Isaacs. After her husband's death and after finishing her children's educating, she dressed in a 'sayal' of coarse cloth and died at the age of one hundred and ten years, begging for alms at the entrance of the door of the Saint Francis's church in Bogota. When asked why she did it, she replied: "In memory of the poorest and most forgotten who live in Chocó, for which my husband fought so much." From these facts, a newspaper from Cali and a Quibdó pamphlet, as a tribute to the memory of both, picked up the news, showing how her life had been more dramatic than that than the novel's heroine she embodied, praising the honesty and the sacrifice of a woman, who after being the First Lady of the nation, had passed, at the end of her life, voluntarily, to poverty, as a gesture of solidarity, with the most forgotten of her homeland.

6

The night Nila arrived in Buenaventura, she didn't know where she would sleep or what would happen to her. She had a deep sadness in her soul and the memory of Barnabas printed on her heart. She thought she would never find a black man like him again. He had sold her his dream like no other and in the time, she had lived with him, she had learned to love him.

On the ship, a nun who came from Cupica to visit her brother, who was bitten by a barracuda, approached her to ask her why she cried and then she told her the tragedy that took place in Playa Huesos and that not everyone knew yet. The frightened nun listened to her and promised to help her as she could and asked that after arriving at the port, she could stay in the convent where she lived, there at least she would be protected from thieves and rapists for some time.

The ship that served the coast, was smuggling goods from Panama and had arrived early, the tide was low, the sea was not so choppy and the breeze came from the north. In front of Cabo Corrientes, two wrecks testified to the dangers caused by the tides. A ship had been stranded on the rocks and a millionaire's yacht had gone to the middle of the jungle and the jungle was devouring it. Two nuns of white coats were waiting for the one that had arrived with Nila and when they heard his story about the massacre, they almost did not believe her, except for a squad of soldiers who came running to the port at that time. They came armed to the teeth, they talked to the captain and asked him to take them immediately to Playa Huesos -Bones Beach-, as the guerrillas had arrived and had not left anyone alive.

On their way to the convent that was on a hill, they had to cross the city. The smell of urine and rancid butter from the fried foods was felt everywhere. Nila came hungry and stopped for a moment to watch what they were selling. Then the nun told her that it was better to hurry and visit the port by day, it was a dangerous place at night and it had so many prostitutes that they no longer fit in some streets, although the last swell, two weeks ago, had drown many and flooded all the hotels on the coast, with the exception of the Station, a Moorish-style building, with openwork in the windows and no glass and that the sea had decided to respect. But not only the swells hit Buenaventura, the criminal gangs too. There were clearly demarcated territories between them, and if one got into the other's territory, they killed him and cut off his head leaving it under the bed of a relative, as a warning. The nun also told her the macabre affair of the "picket houses", which were used to dismember the murdered victims killed by the criminal gangs, then put them in plastic bags and throw them into the sea.

Buenaventura, contrary to its name, had become a small hell, and despite its importance, because 60% of the cargo that entered and left the country moved there, the government had turned a blind eye. Recently a brave journalist had denounced the facts and took a photographer with him to document his story. That act caused the government to send more troops to impose order but it was still too early to know the results. That night, the nuns gave Nila a 'borojó' juice of a dark brown color and good for sleeping and a large piece of goat's cheese.

She was so tired that she didn't even undress. As soon as she lay down on the cot she was given, she fell asleep and in dreams, made love with Barnabas. Next day, newspaper vendors, the radio music of the hundreds of coffee shops and the children's noise playing in the street woke her up with the sun. She had slept well and a bath made her feel better and she began to let go of her sorrows with the water that escaped through a hole in the floor. After breakfast with an orange juice and another piece of cheese and bread, she went out to see her new home. The site was packed with women from all places, because there were many ships anchored, with sailors looking for them. In almost every corner, she observed stalls selling packages of 'chontaduros' - a tropical fruit- with salt, turtle eggs, and crayfish, they were black and small and hung on clusters by its legs, simulating orioles nests and as much as she looked she found no one to sell the juices and the egg muffins like the ones she made, and knew she would have a future there.

7

Two fearful blacks came out to meet him and asked Barnabas if he had anything to trade. He told them he had a pair of rubber boots he no longer needed and two sieves to look for gold. The blacks in return offered him a can of beer, a catfish stew and two bunches of bananas and that seemed enough. He asked if he could spend the night there and they said yes. The one with the least children invited him to his "Tambo" -shack- and lent him a mat. That night it rained incessantly and the roof cans sounded like a 'guacharaca' -

kind of bird- with the downpour, the wind and the rays fell everywhere, but Barnabas slept like a baby. The storms were the same as in the swamp and he had become accustomed to the noise of insects, the rain and the sea waves when he lived on the Pacific coast with Nila and felt like a fish in the water. That was his element and this time he was in it. Outside one could see the 'roofs' supported by guayacán's pillars of almost three meters, some were rectangular, made of palm and other simple unusable canoes, but all were filled with anthill land, forming platforms suitable for cultivation, keeping the seeds planted free of rodents and the 'arrieras ants' that devoured everything. Sometimes when they arrived, they advanced on fronts up to fourteen meters, covering thirty in a minute, but at the same time they produced a detritus from which they fed a fungus that they then ate and that was the best fertilizer. In one of the 'roofs', they cultivated medicinal plants with ancient secrets and in other tomatoes, achiote, onion and chili pepper, a condiment that was not lacking in any of the meals and said that it was good for love and to ward off evil spirits.

The next morning, the rain had stopped and after taking a broth of salted bocachico - fish- and eating a few pieces of fried yucca and a corn 'arepa', that gave him the strength to pass the day. He said goodbye to the whole family and left them five thousand pesos and left-back in search of his raft. Nothing was missing, he climbed on it and continued downstream, leaving his tears behind and Nila's memory farther and farther. The next hamlet would be the Island and below La Grande and on the other side of the next river mouth, was Domingodó. More rivers arrived at the Atrato than Barnabas could count and its course was getting wider and deeper. There he stopped again. It had been a week since he had left the fort. The net had been very useful and in the few times he had thrown it, near any of the banks, he had obtained more fish than he could eat. He tied the raft to a large tree that had been dragged by the current and had stranded on a neighboring shore to the cliff and hid it under its branches' foliage, next to a dead cow that was being eaten by two vultures. No one would look there because of the carrion's smell and he then he walked towards the hamlet.

At that moment, it was when he saw a procession and a priest who threw incense and asked for God's protection against demons. He approached to see what was happening and an old man told him that on the river's other side, entering the mouth of the Domingodó, in a village of the Emberá Catíos Indians, the devil had arrived and that nobody could sleep. When the procession was over, Barnabas approached the priest and introduced himself telling him that he was coming from upstream and that he had once been a sacristan and offered to help him if he wanted to. The priest listened in amazement.

People were so scared of what was happening, that no one left their shacks after six and the children were not attending schools after two of them had disappeared without leaving any trace. According to the gossip, a strange invasion of green flies and some noises like walking under the huts terrified every one. How much of that was true, the priest did not know because he had no one to accompany him to investigate the truth. Barnabas then told him, that he had long wanted to face the devil and knew that he could beat him with his machete if he found him.

That night, they lent him a hammock and hung it on two sticks under a palm shed but it didn't rain. It would be two in the morning when he heard screams across the river, woke up the priest and asked him to get him a flashlight and a canoe. He would have to get there if he wanted me to help him. Something was happening and you had to face the devil or whoever he was, as long as he let him sleep. The priest who was a brave man decided to accompany him and in a boat that was from the parish, equipped with a Johnson engine, began to cross. That night the moon could be seen and the black profiles of the jungle were reflected on the shore.

When they reached the other side, they saw no one and no matter how much they called, nobody answered them. They decided to go up the mouth of the Domingodó, as far as the boat could go, and when they saw a piece of dark beach with the glow of the moon, they climbed it on the shore and continued walking to the Emberá Catíos hamlet, in a covered place through the jungle, next to a stream of crystalline waters that could be heard, when it came down between the palms and the giant `` cranes '' on which the scars perched with their infernal noise. Then the priest explained to Barnabas that in the 'Quechua' language, the word 'Catios' meant 'dark jungle' and that some time ago, all these tribes had built houses in the trees and were man-eating, eating at the end of the battles, the bodies of their enemies killed in combat. The moon illuminated the jungle and the smell of rotten leaves, damp earth and the aromas of thousands of different plants mixed in the air, vivifying the lungs. The Serranía -low mountains- del Baudó that ran parallel to the Pacific coast, separating the valley of the Atrato River from the sea was not very high, with ridges that ranged from 100 to 1,800 m. When they arrived, they began to shout, asking if there was anyone to hear them. An Indian woman breastfeeding her infant was seen in the open area, in front of her cabin. It was circular and was mounted on guayacán's stakes about

151

two meters from the ground and it was climbed by a stick that had notches and which was removed and introduced into the house, in case of danger.

The priest, in his own language, explained why he had gone and if they wanted, he to help them. Soon all the inhabitants of the town began to appear and began to descend from their huts of impeccable manufacturing, built with fine wood and palm roofs until they were completely surrounded and began to tell them what was happening. A woman who had gone for help the day before had not returned and the noises and green flies were still there. Then Barnabas told them to organize groups of three and that he would go in one of them and the priest would go in another, but not before he had blessed the town and poured holy water into each hut. The Indians did not understand that ritual, but they accepted it as long as they helped them.

At the first hint of the devil or some evil spirit, everyone should shout warnings where they had seen him and should run to fight him. This speech seemed to return their courage and each Indian armed himself as he could. They were skilled in hunting and fishing and experts in obtaining poisons, one vegetable they called Pakurú-Niaara, and another that exuded a forest frog were, deadlier than that produced by coral snakes. With those, they had poisoned the chips of their chuspas -bags- in order to shoot the demon with their blowguns. Others were armed with wooden sticks carved with figures of protective spirits and the chief with a shotgun, in addition to his blowgun and his blow with poisoned darts. First, they surrounded the camp and from there they left in all directions. Barnabas entered the crystal-clear water pipe, with a flashlight in his hand and his machete in the other, clearing the manigua -jungle- and the smell of freshly cut branches, vines, and leaves, mixed in the air.

A few minutes after getting into the jungle, following the stream, there was a shotgun shot and screams through the thicket. The Indians were terrified, but Barnabas ran in the direction of the screams and the priest did the same. They arrived at the time and heard a splash and a muffled groan in the middle of a water hole that had formed the rain. Barnabas and the priest shone in the direction of the noise and it was difficult to discover what was happening. The mud splashed their faces and had fallen into their eyes. Suddenly, an immense anaconda poked his head and Barnabas reached to see the chief's body wrapped by the snake, still alive, struggling to get rid of its mortal embrace. Barnabas knew that the animal was fighting for its livelihood, without worrying about who was watching it. As a lightning bolt threw himself into the water and brandishing his machete, he cut off his head from a pit. The rings he had formed around his prey were slowly loosening and the priest pounced on the body of 'Jaibaná' to prevent him from drowning and pulled him to the shore. The animal's body continued to move in violent contractions for two more hours and then began to clear up. Then, between three Indians recovered the snake's body from the pool of bloody water, they measured it by steps and discovered that it was over seven meters and weighed the same as two men. They cracked it from top to bottom with the Barnabas' machete, starting where the head had been and when they reached the middle, where the snake was swollen, they cut the skin and a foul smell and a viscous liquid, leapt into the air bathing the priest's body who had come closer to the corps and there they discovered the bones and skull of a child who had been swallowed whole. No one had doubts about what was happening. They were being attacked by a group of anacondas who had found in that place an easy livelihood and a place to nest and those were the noises below the shacks, which did not let anyone sleep and the rest were their droppings and those of the Indians, visited by green flies.

Before noon they had already found three other snakes, among the leaf litter under the houses and Barnabas had killed them with his machete and when they opened the crop, they had discovered the remains of the other child who had disappeared. However, a woman's body appeared a few days later, shattered against a tree. She had fallen prey to a pack of 'tatabros 'or saínos -wild bores- that had gone down to drink to the river. When she saw them, she got scared and started yelling at them to scared them away and that was when the 'tatabros 'attacked her with her sharp fangs and although she tried to climb a tree, she never succeeded. Her body was shattered as a testimony of her imprudence. That afternoon a celebration was prepared for the two exorcists and roasted two 'tatabros' and some 'guartinajas', 'a pajuil' and two squirrels over low heat and the smoke and the smell of the scorched meat began to rise like an incense in a pagan ritual and Barnabas came to mind the useless sacrifice of his people by the sea.

In his magical ritual, the Jaibaná began to sing, invoking the name of his god called 'Cagarabí' in order to serve as an intermediary to communicate with other high-ranking spirits. His son, he had also learned the profession and was already a healer and instead he was blowing to call the lower spirits, with whom he was taking away the pains of a woman's belly, taking out some worms that had been embedded under her skin. The priest opened his eyes wide when he saw how the worms came out with the blows and prayers of the Indian and since then he applied the same technique, singing psalteries to the sick of his parish when they had scrapie or had been bitten by a poisonous insect. For Barnabas, that was not new, since he had seen the 'nuches' - worms- that were embedded beneath the skin of the zebu cows on the plains of Cesar being expelled by prayers.

Before the end of the celebration, the Jaibaná interrupted his songs and put a necklace to the priest and another to Barnabas, from which jaguar teeth hung and they were both adopted as honorary members of the tribe amid shouts, laughter, and noise copying those of the animals.

8

He felt that his raft was rocking hard with the waves produced by a boat that passed near him. He sat up and heard screams calling his name. He was the captain, who was returning on one of his regular trips between Quibdó and Santa Marta. When he recognized him, he invited him on board and Barnabas did not hesitate. He let go of the raft with the river's sleeping current and with it the aches accumulated in his useless search for lost paradises. He had seen them all closely and had been in them, learning to live the day and not expect anything from him. Hour after hour, minute by minute. He had escaped death so many times that he no longer knew where to start, or where everything would end.

Nothing mattered to him anymore, Nila was left behind and the captain had met her, before dying incinerated in Playa Huesos. She marked a stage, like a clock's pendulum, moving in swings of hope and pain. And so, he was telling the captain on his return trip, how his life had been since he had left them at Vigía del Fuerte and all the pain with Nila's death and things he had seen and learned to do. Two days later, the boat arrived at the port of Zapzurro, where Pablo Escobar once had a house. It could still be seen, it was like a large chalet by the sea, in a very strategic place, with the jungle behind. A couple of hours away, on the other side of a mountain range a few meters high, was the border that separated Colombia from Panama. A lost paradise that could not be taken. He had left many in his useless pursuit of happiness and in his paranoia to hide and also escape. Barnabas had visited another one he had on the beach of Gaira, where they took tourists to show them the useless dreams of a gangster who had everything and had left nothing, just a bad memory and his desire to end all those who They crossed the road. That monument to the ego had been bought by a politician who had been killed in a fight and then his brother had acquired it, or at least that was what they said. It was located in a corner, with two accesses to escape and a gate of steel sheets on the street, which when the wind blew it sounded like it was a soul complaining from the depths of hell.

The boat dropped its anchors in the harbor cove. It was a small town with few houses overlooking the sea. All but the captain, descended to have a beer and get something to eat when they saw her leave the villa that had been Pablo Escobar. It was the last residence Lina had acquired, nobody knew how, or who had bought it, but there she was, dressed in red silk from head to toe and from a distance Barnabas did not recognize her. The good life had gained weight and the face was not the same. Furrows had appeared on her forehead and her hair had been painted another color.

Suddenly a helicopter coming from Capurganá, began to fly over the house, raising clouds of sand from the beach and moving the leaves of the palms and it was when the captain with a megaphone in his hand ordered the pilot to descend and not do any suspicious movement, otherwise, he would be forced to shoot. The pilot smiled in an act of defiance, showing a gold tooth that shone with the sun, and began to lay his ship on the dock in front of the chalet. Lina ran and jumped on the machine and that was when the gunshot of the 50-caliber machine gun was heard and in a matter of seconds, the occupants of the helicopter were injured or had lost their lives, but the engines were still on and the blades continued to spin and a black smoke began to escape from the cabin, being disseminated in the air by the propeller and the turbine rotor. Driven by the hand of fate and his own conscience, Barnabas ran towards the ship, in a heroic act to rescue the crew, from an explosion. As he approached, he saw the pilot with his head thrown back. His mouth was open and he saw a gold tooth shining with the sun. On the other side was Lina, with a gunshot wound that had shattered her shoulder, but in the midst of her pain, she managed to utter a word like a groan of hope: Barnabas! He felt a chill when he heard her voice and withholding the black glasses, he recognized her. In that instant, his life passed before his eyes with the speed of lightning and he remembered the eclipse, the whale's farewell song, the fragility and the hope hidden in the butterfly's blue wings and the Jaibaná's words…

"At the beginning of the road there is the hope for the one who seeks, in the middle, there is the happiness of the one who finds and, in the end, there is sadness of the one who has or loses everything. Beyond sadness, the truth can be seen and when you find it, embrace it. At that moment you can love and remember, it's just an instant, then silence will come, as deep as the sea…"

Their destinies had crossed once more. He hugged her in a vain attempt, trying to free her from her cabin's confinement and that was when the explosion was felt. A ball of fire rose through the air, their bodies flew into a thousand pieces and fell into the sea. The captain could see for a moment, how a shadow eclipsed the sun, and where the helicopter was only a black smoke remained, as an incense and a testimony of their martyrdom.

Map of El Darién and the Atrato River

Printed in Great Britain
by Amazon